More Dog Trouble

Rose Impey and Jolyne Knox

Collins

This edition produced for The Book People Ltd
Hall Wood Avenue, Haydock
St Helens WA11 9UL

Published by A & C Black Ltd in 1994
Published by Collins in 1995
10 9 8 7 6 5 4
Collins is an imprint of HarperCollins*Publishers* Ltd,
77-85 Fulham Palace Road, Hammersmith, London W6 8JB.

ISBN 0 00 763098 0

Text © Rose Impey 1994
Illustrations © Jolyne Knox 1994

The author and the illustator assert the moral right to
be identified as the author and the illustrator of the work.
A CIP record for this title is available from the British Library.
Printed and bound in Great Britain by Omnia Books Limited, Glasgow

The Best Dog in the World

Our dog, Holly, is the best dog
in the whole world.
That's what me and my sister think.
But our dad doesn't.
He's always complaining about her.

4

He tries to pretend
he doesn't like dogs.
But me and my sister think
he just likes to complain.
When we first had Holly it was
moan, moan, moan, all the time.

5

That dog's escaped again.

She gets out sometimes,
no matter how careful we are.
But she *always* comes back.

You can't take her
for walks like a
normal dog.

It's only because
she gets excited
and pulls on her lead.
She doesn't mean
to do it.

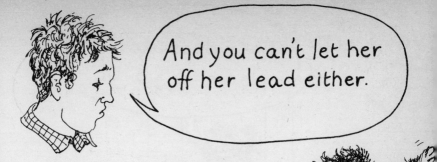

And you can't let her off her lead either.

Well, you can, but if you do she rolls in things.
Dead fish mostly.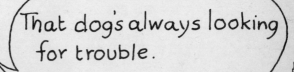

That dog's always looking for trouble.

Sometimes she gets into fights with other dogs.
The trouble is, they're usually bigger than her.

I suppose she is, a bit.
She makes little whimpering
noises at the door, to be let out.
But the minute she's out
she starts whimpering
to come in.

8

And then – when she comes in
– she brings half the garden with her.

The time Dad complained the most
was when Holly got fleas.
Lots of dogs do.
But our dad has gone on about it
ever since.

Quick, get the flea powder.

Well, now we'd got a dog
so it was no use moaning.
As Mum said, 'She's very young.
She hasn't had a proper home before.
She just needs training.'

Then Dad said, 'All right, I'll train her.
We'll see who's boss around here.'

Me and my sister started grinning.
So did Mum, but Dad didn't.
He was dead serious.

'Come on, Holly,' he said.
'We'll show them.'

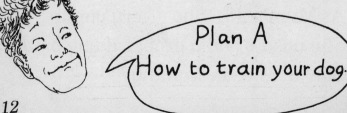

Plan A
How to train your dog.

Dog Training – Plan A

Dad took Holly into the garden.
Me and my sister tried to go with him,
but Dad said,
'You two had better stay inside.
This is serious. It's not a game.'
'Oh, Dad,' we said. 'We want to watch.'

She's <u>our</u> dog.

'You can watch from the window,'
said Dad.
So that's what we did.

Dad took off Holly's lead.
'Sit *down!*' he said,
in a serious voice.
Holly stood
looking up at him.

Dad pushed Holly's
bottom down
to make her sit.
But Holly
stood up again.

Sit,
Holly.
SIT!

Dad pulled a very
serious face.
He pointed a
serious finger.

But Holly jumped up and tried
to lick him.

The more Dad said, '*DOWN!*',
the more Holly jumped *up*.
She thought it was a game.

Me and my sister
started laughing.
Dad looked up at us
so we stopped laughing.
We remembered it was serious.

Next Dad put Holly back on the lead.
He walked Holly up and down the lawn.
Holly kept pulling on her lead.
She looked as if she would
choke herself.

Heel,
Holly
Heel!

Every time Holly
pulled, Dad pulled
her back.

In the end Holly was walking
on her two back legs,
like a circus dog.

Suddenly Holly stopped dead,
but Dad didn't.
He tripped over the lead.

He nearly fell over.
Dad looked up at us.
This time we didn't laugh.
We knew it was serious.

Next Dad made Holly
sit on the grass.
'Now,' said Dad.
'Stay there.'

This time she did
as she was told.
Dad smiled
and looked at us
to make sure
we were watching.
Me and my sister
started clapping.

Good dog!
Well done!

Then Dad found a ball.
He threw it across the garden.
He shouted to Holly,
to bring back the ball.

But Holly just sat there.
So Dad brought it back
to show her what to do.
He threw the ball again.

Fetch!
Bring it to me.

Holly raced around Dad barking.

Her tail wagged excitedly,
but she still didn't fetch the ball.

Dad threw the ball *fifteen* times.
Fifteen times he brought it back.

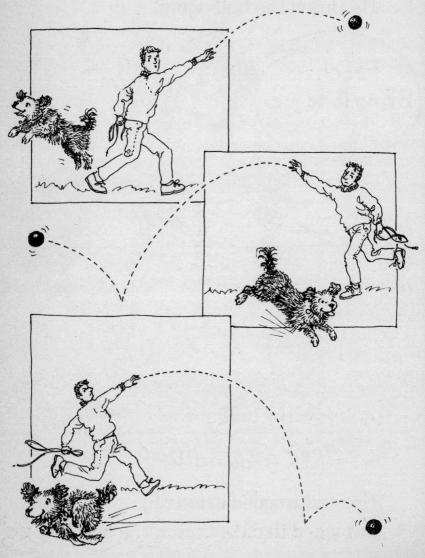

By now Dad had had enough.
He threw the ball down
and walked away in disgust.

He gave up and came in.
He looked tired out.

21

Me and my sister didn't ask him
who was boss.
We didn't say anything.

So much for Plan A.
Anybody else got any
bright ideas?

How about a
cup of tea?

Then Holly came in carrying the ball.
It was covered in mud.

She dropped it at Dad's feet.
Dad closed his eyes
and groaned.

Dog Training – Plan B

While Dad was drinking his tea
Mum said, 'You could try
rewarding her.'
'What for?' said Dad.
'She hasn't done anything yet.'
'Well, when she does.
Dogs like a bit of encouragement.'
'I suppose you mean food,' said Dad.
'She's getting too fat as it is.'

Just titbits,
it's worth a try.

Don't blame me if she
ends up looking like
a roly-poly pudding.

'Oh, Dad,' said my sister.

She rolled Holly over the kitchen
floor and tickled her little
round tummy.
She was getting a bit fatter.
But she wasn't too fat for us.

She's absolutely perfect.

'Humph,' said Dad.
'That's a matter of opinion.'

Over the next week Dad tried to
train Holly, by giving her rewards.
Plan B, he called it.
You won't believe what he gave her.

'Little titbits,' Mum had said.
We knew what she meant:
sweets, the odd biscuit,
a bit of cheese or chocolate buttons.

But that's not what Dad gave her.
He gave her *broad beans!*
Me and my sister *hate* broad beans.

Every time Holly
sat when Dad
told her to,

or came to him
when he
called her,

or walked
without pulling,

he put his hand
in his pocket
and gave her a *bean*!
The amazing thing was
she ate them!
We couldn't believe it.

Holly's a bit of pig really.
She eats almost anything.
She ate so many beans she was sick
all over the kitchen floor.

I think you overdid it. She will get fat at this rate.

Broad beans aren't going to make her fat.

'Not if she sicks them up,' I said.
'I'd sick them up if I had to eat
broad beans,' said my sister.
'That's quite enough of that talk,'
said Mum.

'She's getting fat because
she's getting lazy,' said Dad.
Holly certainly wasn't as lively as
she had been at first.
But we still loved her to bits.
We still thought she was perfect.
But Dad didn't.

'Well, I've had enough,' he said.
'There's only one thing left.'
'What's that?' asked my sister.
'Plan C. Dog Training classes.'
'Great!' I said. 'Can we come?'

Please Dad.
We won't make
a sound.

Dad looked at Mum, then
he looked at us.
'We'll be like mice,'
said my sister.
'Humph,' said Dad.
'We'll see about that.'

Dog Training – Plan C

Monday night, after tea,
we took Holly in the car
to dog training classes.
The hall was full of dogs.
It was . . . brilliant.

Dad didn't think so.
He said it was deafening.

The trainer was called Mr Moore.
He tried to talk above the noise.

Always try to understand your dog. Remember, every dog has its own personality.

It was true. You could see that.
They were completely different.

Jay-Jay, a long-haired
Collie, was so nervous
that his owner
had to carry him in.

Gracie was a thin, nosey,
little Whippet-cross
who *wouldn't* mind
her own business.

Herman was an enormous Great Dane.
He looked like a mountain moving.

Rosco was
a Rottweiler.
He looked fierce
but he was as soft
as custard really.

Baxter was a great big Airedale.
He was like Tigger
in *Winnie the Pooh*.

Baxter couldn't help bouncing.

The most well-behaved
dog was Penny.
Penny was Mr Moore's dog.
She sat as good as gold all night
and didn't move, unless
she was told to.

She's like the teacher's pet.

That's because she is the teacher's pet.

'Everyone line up,' said Mr Moore.
'Take it in turns to walk your dog
down the line.'

Rosco walked all the way
with his head turned
to the side trying to
lick his owner's knees.

Herman moved v - e - r - y
s - l - o - w - l - y.

Gracie sniffed every
dog she passed.
She was so nosey.

Holly walked quite nicely.
She didn't pull.
She didn't drag.
She didn't rush
as if it was a race.

We were proud of her.
Dad said she was
showing off.

But Jay-Jay lay on the floor
like a dead body.
He just *refused* to move.

37

The bit we liked the best
was when Mr Moore told everyone
to make their dogs lie down.

You lie down first
then your dog will
copy you.

Dad didn't like the sound of that.
But he had to do it.

Holly thought it was a great game.

She licked Dad's face
and chewed Dad's ear.

She ran round
and round him.

She jumped over him
as if he was a tree trunk.

This time me and my sister
couldn't help laughing.
It looked like a good
game to us.

At the end of the evening Mr Moore
said the dogs could have a playtime.
It was wonderful.

They all ran round the hall chasing
each other and barking at the tops
of their voices.
It was like the school playground.

Some of the dogs
were bullies and
knocked the other
dogs over.

Some went round
in pairs looking
for more to
make a gang.

Gracie darted about
biting the others
and then
running off.

But Jay-Jay hid
in the corner,
shaking.

Holly wouldn't join in either.
She just sat with us as if she
couldn't be bothered.
Mr Moore came over
and made a fuss of her.

He stroked her and ran his hands
up and down her tummy.
'She's a bit fat, your dog,'
he said to Dad.

'That's what I've been telling them,'
said Dad, 'but they won't listen.
They give her too much to eat.'
Mr Moore laughed.

We couldn't believe our ears.
'What do you mean?' said Dad.
'This dog's five, maybe six
weeks pregnant,' said Mr Moore.
'Didn't you know?'
'No, I did not,' said Dad.

Me and my sister knew how.
We'd learnt all about it at school.
But that's not what Dad meant.

I don't understand.

Does she get out much?

All the time.

The first week we had her she was gone for hours.

'There you are then,' said Mr Moore.
He smiled at us.
'You're going to be far too busy
for dog training classes,' he said,
'with puppies on the way.'

Puppies on the Way

The next day we took Holly
to the vet, just to make sure.
Dad was hoping that Mr Moore
was wrong.
But me and my sister *knew*
he wasn't.

Yes she's having puppies all right. In about three weeks, I'd say.

'Three weeks!' I said.
'*Three weeks!*' said my sister.
'Three weeks,' groaned Dad.

We were so excited we couldn't wait.
The vet told us we must treat her
just the same.

Regular walks but not too far

She must have regular meals but no extras

We must keep her clean and brushed.

And she gave us some vitamins
to make her stronger.

Holly got even fatter
over the next three weeks.
We could feel the bumps
in her tummy.

I can
count twelve.

'Twelve!' said Dad.
'No, don't worry, Dad,' I said.
'It says here,'

The litter: the average number of puppies in a litter is five or six.

'*Five or six*,' said Dad.
'Is that supposed
to make me feel better?'

'Where will we keep them all?'
said my sister.
Her eyes grew big and excited.

'Don't think about it,' said Dad.
'But Dad . . .' we said.

Now listen
to me.
We've got a dog already.
One dog is enough
for this family.
We are not keeping
<u>any</u> puppies.
Don't even think
about it.

Me and my sister opened our mouths
to speak. Mum shook her head.
We knew what that meant.
Not now, don't ask *now.*
So we didn't.
We could wait.

Holly had her puppies on a Friday,
a school day.
Can you believe our Dad made us
go to school?

It was the longest day
we'd ever had.

When we came out of the school gate
Mum was waiting by the car.

'Jump in,' she said. 'Holly's started
having her puppies.'

When we got there it had
all happened.
I felt so fed up to have missed it.
But when I saw Holly,
licking a little black shape,
I was so excited
I just wanted to cry.

She was surrounded by them.
Five tiny puppies.
They were soft and wet
and their eyes were still closed
so you couldn't tell
which end was which.
They looked like a
bundle of sausages.

'Holly seems different,'
said my sister.

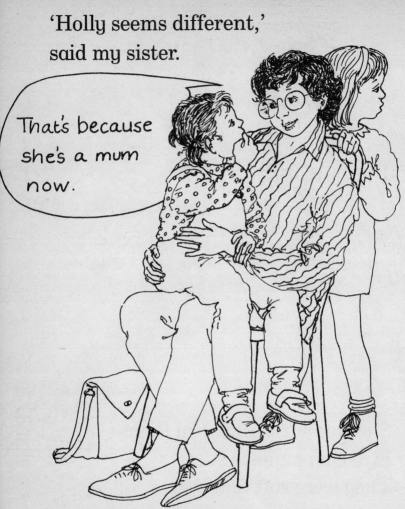

That's because she's a mum now.

It felt funny, Holly being a mum.
She didn't seem old enough.
The vet said she was a good mum.
She looked after her puppies
really well.

'No,' said the vet. 'It's instinctive.
Animals just know what to do.
But some are better at it.'
We were so proud of Holly.

At first the puppies looked
exactly the same.
But over the next few weeks,
when they started moving about,
we could tell they were different.
We each had our favourite.

61

Even Dad couldn't resist them.
There was a really tough little one
that kept getting itself into scrapes
and having to be rescued.
Dad called him 'Bruiser'.

One time we caught Dad
playing with Bruiser.
He saw us watching him.

Before you ask
the answer's no.
N---- O ---- no.
We are not keeping
<u>any</u> of these
puppies.
Certainly not.
Out of the question
Absolutely----no..
no .... no .... no..
---- N O !

Me and my sister thought we had
heard that somewhere before.
He *sounded* as if he meant it.
But we just smiled.
We weren't going to give up
that easily.